T0209224

THE PROTECTORS OF EMPERIA

THE PROTECTORS OF EMPERIA

The Five Elements

GIOVANNI UZOKWE

THE PROTECTORS OF EMPERIA
THE FIVE ELEMENTS

iUniverse books may be ordered through booksellers or by contacting:

iUniverse
1663 Liberty Drive
Bloomington, IN 47403
www.iuniverse.com
844-349-9409

ISBN: 978-1-6632-2197-1 (sc)
ISBN: 978-1-6632-2196-4 (e)

Library of Congress Control Number: 2021909876

Print information available on the last page.

iUniverse rev. date: 04/30/2021

To my mom, who I love dearly

CHAPTER ONE

The gleaming quartz building seemed to cascade over Sabrina as she stood on the rocky path leading towards Wolfighter.

Rainbow roses sprinkled the grass, their delicate petals seeming to calm everything around them. Sabrina watched as a sapling poked its head out of the ground, surprised that it grew so quickly, soon turning into a rose identical to the others. Sabrina's mom must have spotted where she was looking because she said, "When we plant the seeds, we use a unique liquid called Tealium. Tealium has a special chemical that produces pure water and life, letting the plant grow quicker than any human plant. We only plant them in spring because they represent that everybody is unique. That everybody has their likes and dislikes." *No wonder!* Sabrina thought. She had come to Emperia in the summer and had only lived there for a month. She hadn't realized it was spring yet. Sabrina couldn't help but stare as another sapling morphed into a beautiful multicolored rose with blue-tipped leaves

Sabrina's mom shook her out of her daze. "You need to stop staring into space like that. Your session starts in twenty minutes."

"Who's my mentor?" she asked, crossing her fingers and hoping it was a good one.

"Mr. Tucker."

At that, her eyes lit up. Even though she'd only seen the mentor once, he had always been nice to her. He had once tried to save her from teleporting to the Moonbeams layer. He had even gathered the other mentors to find out where she had gone to try and see if they could save her. But her face immediately fell when her mom added, "Amethyst will be there too." Sabrina groaned.

Amethyst was her arch-enemy. She hadn't greeted her with any warm "hello!" or "how are you doing?" when Sabrina had started at Wolfighter, but instead with a note that read "Loser" in big fine print. From then on, Sabrina had hated her.

Especially when she had shown up with her gang and started blabbering her mouth off about how Level Five was 'her' grade and everything. Though, Sabrina had gotten her back for that.

"Why does she have to be there?" Sabrina mumbled, wishing that she could throw something at the marble statue that seemed to be snickering at her as she passed.

"Because she has the same power as you." "And that is..." Sabrina pressed.

Sabrina's mom sighed as she said, "She also can shape-shift like you."

Sabrina's jaw dropped. Amethyst hadn't told her that she could shape-shift.

Sabrina swallowed a mouthful of bile. Was that what Amethyst had meant when she had mouthed, I'll get you back? Sabrina hadn't thought of that.

"Is there a problem?" Sabrina's mom asked, raising an eyebrow.

"Nothing," Sabrina said. Maybe a *little* too quickly.

Her mom didn't look convinced but didn't say anything. Instead, she just sighed and twisted the emerald fabric on her garment.

"I still don't get why you're wearing that," Sabrina said for the millionth time. When her mom didn't answer, Sabrina asked, "Is there something important I need to know?"

"Not until the time is right." Sabrina sighed.

"I figured you would be less than surprised with my answer," Her mom said, staring at anywhere but Sabrina.

"You know me too well," Sabrina said as a smile crept up her lips. Her mom could be strict, but she always seemed to make things better.

Her mom stopped so abruptly that Sabrina bumped into her back.

"Oww," she complained, rubbing her sore nose.

"Sorry,"

Sabrina shrugged. It didn't hurt that much. But the pain went away as her mom opened the incarnate gold doors to Wolfighter. The breathtaking gleaming walls and crisscrossing stairs blanketed with a red carpet always seemed to make everything better as prodigies in orange cloaks passed, one of them glancing at Sabrina and smiling. She smiled back.

Without hesitation, Sabrina ran up the stairs and. . .

. . .bumped into her best friend, Marigold.

Marigold had been her best friend on the first day she arrived at Wolfighter. She had introduced her to people, and that way, more people wanted to get to know her. They had become best friends forever on that day. "Sorry," Sabrina said, rubbing her now extra sore nose now that she had bumped it again. She gasped when she saw her friend's golden dress and midnight choker. Her hair was pulled back in a bun (as usual), and it looked like she had put two layers of pink lip gloss on.

"Meh, it's okay. So how do I look?" she said, twirling around and showering Sophie with tiny flecks of golden dust. Sabrina rubbed the flecks out her eyes before she said, "You look...beautiful," she said, trying not to stare at the glittering rubies clipped to her hair.

"I do? At first, I thought about adding a tiara on top, but then I changed my mind." "Actually, I think you would look good with a tiara," Sophie said, wanting to get away as fast as she could so she could escape to her dorm.

"You do? Ok, wait here. I have a surprise for you." She swirled around, showering Sabrina with more flecks of gold. When Sabrina opened her eyes, she was gone. "So much for trying to escape,"

Sabrina grumbled, dusting the rest of the gold flecks off her cloak. She waited for two minutes before her friend reappeared in a flash of blinding light. She had a silver tiara with red rubies engraved into it.

Somehow she looked even more breathtakingly beautiful as she handed Sabrina a golden box.

"Sorry I took so long. I had to wrap it to perfection, so it looked like part of the box."

Marigold was right. It did look like part of the box to her. But now that Sabrina knew it wasn't, it didn't like it *at all*.

"Thank you," Sabrina said, starting to unwrap the paper.

"Uh, uh," Marigold said, grabbing her arm to stop her from unwrapping it all the way, "no peeking. I mean it. I don't want to spoil the surprise. I bet you don't want to spoil it either. Do you?"

"No," Sabrina admitted. She could wait a *little* bit longer.

"Ok, how about you can open it when you get to your dorm. Deal?"

"Deal."

Marigold let out a sigh. "Thank you." "No problem."

Sabrina turned and started walking down the hallway before she remembered something. Just as Marigold was turning the corner, Sabrina yelled, "Why is everybody wearing dresses?"

Marigold smiled as she said, "for the Springtide Ceremony."

CHAPTER TWO

~~~~~◆~~~~~

*S*pringtide Ceremony? Sabrina thought as she walked back to her dorm room. *Was that what her mom was hiding from her this whole time? She knew she loved ceremonies. Why would her mom hide it from her?* Sabrina thought as she opened her door to her dorm room. She pushed the thought away as she entered her dorm and looked around. Everything was intact and in place. Her emerald bed stood in all its prominent glory, matching pillows and blanket, adding the finishing touch. Her reading corner with her spellbook was a little dusty, and Sabrina made a mental note to clean it after the ceremony. Right now, she needed to find what to wear. And it had to be good. She caught a glimpse of light near her bandstand. She couldn't help but smile as her emerald wand came into view. She quickly thought of a spell which was, in fact, the shortest spell she had ever thought of, promptly grabbed her wand and pointed it at herself, chanting, "Make my dress the fanciest yet!"

A flurry of sparks shot out of her wand and surrounded her in a blinding flash of light. The light soon cleared, and the sparkles died. Sabrina quickly ran over to the mirror in her bathroom. She nearly fainted when she saw her dress. She wore an emerald dress that glowed in the dim lights of the bathroom. An emerald choker with a ruin in the middle was clasped around her neck. Matching emerald earrings hung from her ears, and she wore emerald platform boots with golden laces.

"Wow," she whispered. She looked perfect in the dress. But there was something off about it. Then she remembered. Quickly, she ran to her bed stand where the golden box was, still wrapped in the golden paper and nothing out of place.

Please be emerald; please be emerald, please be emerald, she thought as she tore at the paper. She took a deep breath before she opened the box. She almost jumped as she noticed a silver tiara with three emeralds embedded into it. Running back to the bathroom, she adjusted the tiara on her head.

"There," she said, "all done." She grabbed her wand and spellbook before running out of her dorm and to her session.

"You look beautiful," Mr. Tucker said as soon as she stepped foot in the room.

"Thank you. Sabrina said, swirling around and dipping an elegant curtsy.

He smiled. "You used magic?"

Sabrina nodded. "I didn't have any good dresses from the human world."

"Well," he said, turning to a window that had a great view of Emperia with its lush meadows and trees. "I suppose you're ready to start your session?"

"Yeah, but where's Am-"

"Right here," a familiar voice said as the door opened. Amethyst stepped in. She wore a cream-colored dress with chrysanthemums attached to her yellow sash. When she saw Sabrina's dress, she gasped and covered her mouth. Quickly changing her mood, she glared at Sabrina and spat, "What are you looking at?" Sabrina was about to shout a mean retort before Mr. Tucker said, "Now, now, Amethyst. We don't want any quarrels here in this session. You can save that for later. Understood?" He waited until they both nodded before he continued, "Good. I am sure you've heard that you two will be doing your sessions together from now on?"

"Now on!?" yelled Sabrina and Amethyst at the same time.

Mr. Tucker smiled. "I know you guys might be rivals, but you still need to bond and work together. That is one of the most critical things in magic. But today, I'll have to teach you the rules of shape-shifting."

Sabrina groaned as he snapped his fingers, and then a vast book appeared that looked like it would take years to read. So, Sabrina spent the rest of the session listening to the most boring lecture she had listened to, and Amethyst just had to make it worse by glaring at her and giving her a huge pathetic smirk that made Sabrina want to punch her in the face.

At the end of the session, Sabrina stumbled out of the room. Her legs ached, and her eyes hurt from glaring at Amethyst so many times. She ran down the hallway and sat down on the stairs. Then somebody called her name. Her head shot up. Someone was waving at her. It was Simon!

Simon was one of her first friends ever in the human world before Miles came along. They had come to Emperia to stay away from Mrs. Crane. Their human teacher who planned to take their powers from them.

Sabrina jumped up from her spot and jetted down the stairs. She ran over and hugged him.

"You look beautiful," said Simon, pulling away to admire her. Sabrina blushed and looked at her feet. "You look handsome too."

He wore a red tuxedo and had a white bow. His hair was gelled to perfection, and a strong scent of cologne radiated off him.

He shuffled his feet. "Thanks," he said, reaching for her hand then quickly drawing it back.

"Where's Miles?" she said, wanting to change the subject as fast as she can.

"Oh, he's still at his session. Apparently, Mrs. Tira thinks he's starting to get good at understanding the similarities and differences between nature and darkness." he smiled as he added, "I think he's enjoying it a lot."

Sabrina raised an eyebrow.

Simon noticed it and said, "She's a mentor that teaches nature and other abilities."

Sabrina nodded but tried to imagine Miles listening to a long list of similarities and differences. He hated listening to rules. But he seemed to like this one.

"Anyway," said Simon, shuffling his feet, "we're supposed to pick one partner for the ceremony so we can get to know each other more, and I was wondering-" his voice trailed off, and he shuffled his feet again before he added, "you'd be my partner?"

Sabrina took a second to process what he was saying.

"Ah-I- sure!" she stammered as she felt her face heat up.

"Really? Thank you. I was wondering if you'd say no." he blushed and quickly said, "I heard you had a session with Amethyst. How was it?"

Sabrina filled him in about how the mentor had given her a long lecture about the rules of shape-shifting and how Amethyst had kept glaring at her the whole time.

"Wow," he said, "looks like you guys had a pretty interesting time." He smiled when Sabrina rolled her eyes.

"Ready for lunch?" Simon said. "Totally."

"Race ya!" he said, then jetted off.

Sabrina followed.

The cafeteria was humongous. Just as Sabrina had remembered. Golden chandeliers hung from the ceiling. About fifty tables were covered with a linen cloth that shimmered when somebody passed by. Beautiful maids passed by from their cafeteria, where they made their delicious food. The mouth-watering smell of delicious food wafted around the cafeteria. Sabrina ran toward the cafeteria line and topped her plate with foods from A to Z. She sat down next to Simon because her parents were not there. "Wow," Simon said. "Do you think it's a good idea to stuff yourself before the ceremony?"

"I don't know," Sabrina said between mouthfuls of spaghetti.

"You sound like a pig," Simon said, laughing and snorting.

"Look who's laughing," said Sabrina, mimicking the snorting sounds Simon was making.

That only made them burst out in more laughter.

"Look at the losers, laughing like hyenas," said Amethyst tying her hair into a ponytail.

Sabrina's head shot up. She wasn't surprised when she saw Amethyst and her two friends Theodora and Minerva, standing over her and cackling like witches.

"Leave us alone, Amethyst," she said, doing her best not to make her fly across the room. One of Sabrina's powers was the ability of telekinesis. If she wanted, she could make Amethyst hit the ceiling nine times and not run out of energy.

"Right. Like, I'll do that. I came here to do something else that is way more important than leaving you alone." Her wicked smile made it evident that, whatever she was doing, was *not* going to be good. At all.

CHAPTER THREE

—◆—

Amethyst whirled around in a flashing light. Sabrina quickly shielded her eyes. Simon shook her shoulder. "Um, Sabrina? You might want to look."

Sabrina slowly opened her eyes. A growling lion with sharp claws and teeth stood in front of her. A shaggy orange mane practically covered the lion's face, but she could still spot the piercing eyes that studied Sabrina like it was ready for a tasty snack. Sabrina slowly backed away.

"Nice lion, I'm not too much of a delicious meal."

"Well, what are you waiting for?" Amethyst-er, the lion growled. "Come on, shapeshift into something." The lion pounced, and Sabrina screamed and jumped out of the way.

"Hey," said Simon, jumping out and blocking Amethyst from going any further. "Do NOT touch her.

"What are you going to do?" the lion growled with a hint of mock in her voice.

Simon closed his eyes. "Bor-" before she could finish her sentence, she was interrupted by a rolling sphere of water. It quickly sucked up the lion into the sphere, leaving the lion hopelessly wheezing and gasping for air. Then, it spun around, shapeshifting into a whale. But she still couldn't get out of the bubble.

"Simon . . . stop!" Sabrina yelled. Simon carefully lowered the sphere and parted the water, letting Amethyst, who was now back to her regular self, collapse in a shaky mess on the floor.

"What is going on here!?" said Mrs. Kristine, the principal of Wolfighter, as she strode in with a rainbow-colored dress and matching bracelets. Everyone in the cafeteria pointed shamelessly at Amethyst. "Amethyst, what did you do?" Mrs. Kristine said, leaning over Amethyst and staring at the lump that looked very much like Amethyst. Suddenly, Amethyst jumped up and pointed her shaking finger at Sabrina and Simon. "LOOK AT WHAT THEY DID TO MY DRESS!" she yelled—waving at her now wrinkled dress. *It makes her look like a rag doll,* thought Sabrina. As a smirk peppered her lips. "AND LOOK AT HER!" Amethyst continued yelling, "SHE DOESN'T HAVE THE RIGHT TO BE SMIRKING AT ME LIKE THAT! SHE'S GUILTY TOO!" Then she collapsed in a heap on the floor and started crying again.

Principal Kristine rolled her eyes. "Detention." Which only made Amethyst cry even louder. "Ok," she said, turning to them, "spill it. What actually happened?"

So Sabrina ended up telling Mrs. Kristine all that had happened. About how Amethyst had promised to get vengeance on her. And how she had started fighting and how she ended up in a bundled heap on the floor. Mrs. Kristine decided to send Amethyst to detention still and dismissed lunch early. Simon said goodbye to Sabrina and promised to meet her at the ceremony. Sabrina ran into her room, took a good shower before changing back into her dress again, and ran outside where the ceremony would be held.

The sight was beautiful. Red and white and golden streamers were hung in the air, and the sky seemed to be glowing with multicolored rays. Then Sabrina noticed that they were the rainbow-colored flowers that her mom had shown her earlier in the morning. *Wow,* Sabrina thought. There were Buffet tables with delicious foods like cookies and ice cream with lemonade and other goodies. The ground was littered with the sight of gold and orange confetti. As she passed, she could see people laughing and telling jokes to each other. She tried to spot Simon in the crowd but couldn't find him. Instead, she saw Miles.

"Miles!" she yelled. He spotted her right away. The exciting thing was that he had picked her BFF Marigold to be his partner.

"Wow! You look handsome.." "Thanks," said Miles. But I still think that this tuxedo is a little too scratchy. He scratched his neck, where a red bruise had formed.

Marigold and Sabrina laughed. But before Miles could spit back a retort, a loud voice boomed over the sounds of laughter and the noisy gulping as the boys challenged each other to see who could chug down their lemonade first.

"Welcome to the *SPRINGTIDE CEREMONY!*" Suddenly, Mrs. Kristine appeared, seeming to be walking on thin air. There was a round of applause and laughter. Even the boys had stopped chugging down their drinks. Parents stopped talking, and everyone quieted down. "I am so happy to be here today at this ceremony! There was another round of applause. "As you know," she continued, "this is an annual celebration that we hold every year. I am delighted to pronounce that today is Wolfighter's one-thousandth anniversary!" There was a fit of emotional tears and laughter and clapping as fluorescent lights covered the place in an orange glow. *Why is everybody so emotional?* Sabrina thought. Golden confetti fell from the sky, and people jumped and twirled, full of happiness.

Sabrina had no choice but to play along. Simon walked up next to her.

"Great party, huh?" he asked. "Yeah."

He waited for a moment before he asked, "Would you care for a dance?"

Sabrina considered this, and she started blushing like crazy.

"Um . . . sure?" Sabrina said, realizing she had just accepted to dance with Simon. She looked around. She could spot two people, only two people dancing.

Marigold and Miles. Why couldn't she do it? It was just dancing, after all. She cleared her throat.

"Sure," she said in a clearer and more of a sure voice.

"Great," Simon said, taking her hand in his. They tangoed and twirled into the night until their legs went limp. Simon and Miles rested on a side bench as Marigold and Sabrina chatted away.

"So, how did you turn out to be Miles's partner?" Sabrina asked.

"Oh, it was the best!" Marigold started. "About an hour or two after you left to get ready for the ceremony, he came out of Mrs. Tira's dorm, and once he saw me, he asked if I would be his partner for the ceremony. I literally almost jumped out of my gown. That was the best part today.

You?" Sabrina told her her story of how Simon had asked to be her partner and how she'd accepted. Their stories were almost alike.

"Want to get some drinks and sweets?" Marigold asked, having nothing else to say.

"Uh . . . sure, "Sabrina said. "We can get some for Simon and Miles too. Sabrina said, having sympathy for them. They stood up and walked towards the tables. The boys had resumed chugging down their drinks, and they had to dodge past them so they wouldn't get sprayed on.

They approached a sign that read:

BUFFET TABLE! EAT AS
MUCH AS YOU WANT!

Marigold quickly ran over and got four drinks, handing four vanilla cupcakes for Sabrina to carry. They walked back to the boys.

They seemed to be in deep conversation when they reached them. Miles looked up and smiled at them. "Thanks," he said as they handed him and Simon refreshments, "We were just talking about My session with Mrs. Tira. She was actually very nice, and when she heard that we had moved into the Fifth Level, she got all jittery and excited. Then she tested me on all kinds of stuff. I got really good at it, and she was so proud and excited that she decided to let me have a book that she had preserved over the years. And she gave me this book," he said, pointing to a book that Simon was analyzing with such intention that Sabrina wondered if he was actually reading it or just looking at the pictures that appeared probably in every single inch and corner of the page and only a few diminutive descriptions of the images here and there. The book's binding was filthy, and there was a short gash running down along the spine. Some of the pages had a few stains on them. It must be ancient. Other pages were filled with sand and grime. Sabrina almost grimaced. It looked so discarded and out of order. She waited until Simon handed it two her, and she flipped it over to look at the cover. The title of the book was called The Five Elements.

CHAPTER FOUR

The five elements? It sounded so familiar yet not so familiar at all. She opened the first page and scanned it. There was a picture with five stones, each of their own color. They seemed to be rotating around a golden V. That was probably a Roman numeral, which stood for five. And behind all of that stood a light background of the Earth. But the thing that Sabrina was so startled by was that the pictures were actually moving! Well, except the V. But, other than that, the earth and stones were constantly spinning around so fast that, after watching it for a while, it became a light background. Just a blurred picture of blue, green, and a lot of multi-colors. It abruptly stopped, and then words seemed to write themselves on the page:

When the happiest of times comes to an end and trouble starts to brew, you'll have to find five gemstones to mend hidden under stones and fallen dew. You must learn patience and peace to complete this task and seek a wizard that knows the future and past. You must restore the peace in the future; alas, Emperia will remain in the dark, gloomy, past

Sabrina nearly dropped the book. That sounded like a prophecy. A prophecy she knew rather well. However, she couldn't quite place it. Marigold realized the expression on her friend's face and moved closer. The words were rewriting themselves on the page as if it wasn't impressed with them. Marigold's eyes widened. "The Moonlit Prophecy," she whispered. Simon seemed to have overheard them. "Did you say the Moonlit Prophecy?" Marigold bit her lip and grabbed the book. "No, no, no," she muttered, flipping through the pages. She pulled out a silk handkerchief and dabbed her face.

Sabrina thought that was kind of funny, but she pursed her lips and tried to resist the urge to laugh.

Sabrina pointed to the page with the logo (it was a good name for it), and she watched as Marigold's eyes moved swiftly across the page, though she could see her right eye starting to form a twitch.

"Know anything?" Sabrina asked; she was growing impatient now; she wanted answers IMMEDIATELY.

"This is a prophecy that most little children get told at bedtime here. I remember my mom did the same thing to me. This was a prophecy written by our only true prophet, Tim Starlight. He's still alive and P&P.

"P&P?" Simon asked, for he was listening to their conversation too.

Marigold shifted in her gown. "Popular and Powerful. We respect all P&P's enormously. Sadly, we haven't had any of them in years, and it's decreasing our culture immensely.

Sabrina was Interested now. "Where does this Tim Starlight live?"

Marigold pursed her lips as if this was something she wasn't supposed to tell.

"I . . . Come over to my house tomorrow. I think my dad knows a thing or two about this specific subject. He works with an association that is investigating him."

Sabrina nodded, still thinking. She took the book back from Marigold and started scrutinizing its pages. "I wonder if there's any clue in here that will help us figure out this prophecy."

"Yeah," Miles said, "but first, I think I'm going to take a little nap."

Sabrina agreed. She said goodbye to Simon, Miles, and Marigold, and then headed off to the school. She thought as she opened the door and then took her time to walk up all the 100 flights of stairs. She needed time to think. *I need more information about Tim Starlight. But I don't know where to get the info! Hmm . . . Wait a second, is there a library in here?*

Maybe there is one! There has to be a library here, of course. This is a school! I just need someone to help me. Then an idea clicked in her head. She knew how to teleport from her other classes. Now, readers, don't get all jealous about this 'teleportation' thing. It hurts. Like crazy.

So even if you can in the future, DO NOT DO IT.

She remembered the instructions Mr. Tucker had told her, and then she closed her eyes and concentrated. At first, she didn't feel anything at all. But then, she felt a tingling all over her body and then opened her eyes. She was no longer on the stairs but in her bedroom. She smiled and thought of something to do. Then she remembered the album of her when she was little that she had cast with a spell.

She got it from her nightstand and opened it up. The first picture she saw was Miles, Simon, and her, in little diapers. She had remembered that moment when they had first had a playdate in her house. *That* was a good memory. She flipped the page and saw them when they were three, hiking with her mom. They all loved to hike.

Every day her mom had off from work, they would go out into the woods and frolic and play around until night. But that was until she ended up in this world . . . she stared at the picture for a moment and then shifted her eyes to the following picture. She caught her breath.

CHAPTER FIVE

⸻◆⸻

There she was, in kindergarten maybe, drawing a picture of the exact same logo she had seen on the book before. What the heck? What was that doing here? She stared at it closely. She was a cluttered drawer at that time, but she knew it was the logo. Those squiggly lines were an exact resemblance to the logo. She could see the diamonds and pearls and gems rotating around the

Roman numeral. If she could just figure out what it meant, she'd probably solve the clue to the prophecy. But why would she be drawing that logo? Actually, how was she drawing that picture? She didn't even know what it even looked like. Something clicked in the back of Sabrina's head, but she couldn't quite wrap her head around it. Wait a second; she wasn't even in the library!

How was she even here? How hadn't she realized that before? She was supposed to be in the library in the first place. So she concentrated and concentrated until her mind barely busted. She was going to need a lot of energy for this. She pushed the energy out of her mind, and then she felt a warm tingling all over her body.

When she opened her eyes, she was at the front doors of the library. She tucked the album under her arm and opened the door. There was no light on, so she felt around the walls for a light switch. She found it and clicked it on. She viewed her surroundings. There were stacks upon stacks upon stacks upon stacks of books. The library shelves were outlined with gold, maybe fake, and there was a ladder to climb up to the higher shelves for books. There was only one table that was about the size of a stool with extra stuffing. The library looked all dusty and dirty. They might have even been there for hundreds and thousands of years. The floorboards of the place groaned under her feet. Shades were covering the windows, so she lifted them and peeked out the windows. She could hear the chattering as people cleaned up the remains and wrappers from the ceremony. She shifted her focus on what she was there for. She went to the T section and scanned the bookshelves. "T-a, T-b, T-c, . . T-j, T-i!" She scanned the section, but she didn't find any title that had Tim Starlight on it. She was just about to give up when she saw a dusty book, similar in shape and size to the book with the runes on it. The title was covered in grime and sand, so she dusted it off with her sleeve. And her luck! It was a biography of Tim Starlight, written by Tim himself! She breathed a sigh of relief and then found herself at a comfy table. Well, not *really* comfortable, as her arms would repeatedly slip off the pad every nanosecond. She got tired of trying to read all over the darn place and just decided to give her eyes a rest. Probably just for a little while . . .

CHAPTER SIX

———◆———

S abrina wasn't surprised when she woke up to a lady with shiny gray hair and spectacles. She wore a leather jacket with gold trim. On her wrist hung a golden charm bracelet, minus the charms. For sure, no "charm" would cheer this lady up. She wore a pair of jeans and designer high heels. She had amber eyes, which were fascinating yet scary. Her face was scrunched up in an *I-don't-know-what-the-hell-ya-little scumbug-is-doin'-here,-but-if-ya-don't-g et-that-dirty-butt-of-yours-out-of-here,-I'm callin-security* face.

Unfortunately for her, those were the exact words she said.

Her voice was cold yet sharp and bold.

Sabrina felt like she could die of embarrassment right there.

"Well, um . . . I was just, uh, leaving madam. Sorry." She was about to stand up when the lady put a bony hand on her shoulder.

"Wait. You must've come for something. No one comes here unless they need or want information on an important topic."

Sabrina wasn't so sure she wanted this lady to get into her business, but she had no choice. This *was* the librarian; after all, she might have some information on Tim. She picked up the book and handed it to the lady.

"What's your name?" she asked. If this lady was going to get into *her* business, she would get hers too.

"The name's Melissa. And yours?"

Not fair.

"Sabrina."

"Well, fortunately for you, darling, I know this specific person. This book he wrote is a fake. He is never willing to share any of his secrets."

"That might not be true, though."

"It IS true. I've LIVED the truth. I am his sister."

Sabrina couldn't tell if she was telling the truth or not. Her expression never changed. Her eyes studied Sabrina in a way that made Sabrina want to glare right back. She felt irritated for some reason. She didn't know why, though.

"You—" She took a deep breath as she felt the hatred lift off her like a weight. "Then will you help me with this, um—report?" Melissa's eyes turned dark, and she spoke in a mysterious voice. "THIS IS NO REPORT. YOU WANT TO FIND OUT WHERE THE GEMSTONES ARE."

Sabrina yelped and backed away from her. *What the heck is happening?* she thought. Melissa suddenly stopped, and her eyes turned back to normal. "Excuse me. I don't know what just came over me." Sabrina nodded on the outside, but on the inside, she wanted to get out there as fast as she could. "How—What . . ." she was speechless. How did Melissa know what she was thinking?

Melissa straightened her leather jacket. "I can read minds. An ancient and rare ability. Very useful."

Sabrina did *NOT* want anybody poking around in her head. "Would you mind not using it on me?" she asked.

Melissa smirked and said, "Depends." Sabrina wanted to slam the book down on the librarian's head. "Look—"

"I'm looking," Melissa said. Sabrina scowled.

"Would you just help me with this r—er, prophecy?"

Melissa clicked her tongue. "Every bargain comes with a payment, darling."

Who does this woman think she is? She thought. *Aren't librarians supposed to be nice?*

"And . . ."

"Five gemstones. Or, should I say, The Five Elements?"

Sabrina's eyes widened. She was talking about the gemstones from the prophecy: 'you'll have to find five gemstones to mend hidden under stones and fallen dew.'

She was reading her mind. She was stealing information from her one-by-one. Sabrina didn't want to give it to her. But she needed the information. "Fine. Now tell me where the gemstones are."

CHAPTER SEVEN

———◆◆◆———

S abrina left the library with a lot of information. She carried five files, *probably for each gemstone,* she thought and was anxious to open them. Melissa had told her not to open them until she had as much information as she needed. She *did* have enough information, she thought well, she still needed to meet up at Marigold's house, maybe she would receive more information from Marigold and her father, though she did not know how much time she had left, nor what time she was supposed to meet. Maybe at lunch, then? She patted her back pocket to check for her wand. Darn. She had left it in her dorm. Anyway, she needed to hurry up, or she'd lose her session with her mom. It was for the ability to balance the energy of her powers. She hurried frantically to her dorm and set the files on her desk. She grabbed her wand and changed into her school attire. She knew the way around some of the castle now since she'd been there for more than three months. She trudged down the stairs as she headed to her lesson. When she came to the main entrance, or rather, Grand Entrance, she sat down to relax her tired legs. She sat there for a moment and decided that she should get up when the school bell rang once, the warning that the field was available to anyone. She needed to get going.

Despite her aching legs, she ran to the field. It was a vast place, full of people wickedly using their powers and abilities to freeze and torment people—actually kind of fun. The ground had a safety measure. Anybody that got hit by a spell or injured got safely and quickly revived. She had never tried it, though. She ran across the field to where her mom was waiting. Simon and Miles weren't there yet, but she sat on the bench next to her mom and fiddled with her dress.

She still had to shower, but she did not have enough time to do it yet. She tried to take her mind off the Moonlit Prophecy and asked her mom, "You weren't at the ceremony yesterday. Why?" Her mother sighed. I had so many things to do. Plus, I didn't want to interrupt your dat—dance with Simon. Sabrina frowned with a hint of disapproval. She swore her mother had almost meant to say date.

Grownups.

She playfully rolled her eyes and opened a book she had brought, information on Tim. Just as she was about to start, Simon and Miles showed up.

"What took you guys so long?" she asked, looking down at her watch. Five whole seconds had passed—what a waste of time. Miles frowned at her. "We were right on time."

"Yet late by nine—ten whole seconds." He rolled his eyes and sat down on the bench next to her. He set his things down, and Simon did the same. Sabrina was sorry for behaving like an idiot to her friends, but her mind was too focused on Tim Starlight even to care. "Today, I will teach you how to control the ability to balance the energy of your powers. This is a tough lesson to learn, I'll warn you. Be prepared.

Concentrate. Now, who would like to go first? Oh right. Let me show you how to control. It first. The first thing you have to do is—," Suddenly, her watch beeped, and she disappeared. It took Sabrina a second to figure out what had happened. It was probably her mom's coworkers trying to get hold of her. Well, she guessed that canceled the lesson for the day. Sadly, she was looking forward to learning how to control her powers. Well, with more stabilizability. Miles and Simon looked shocked too, and she explained to them what had happened. After that, they all nodded and decided to go something else. That basically meant they had spare time to do whatever they wanted to do. Therefore, Sabrina could maybe go and look into the files or do something more useful. Oh!

MPerhapsshe was supposed to meet Marigold now! She ran as fast as her legs could take her to

Marigold's dorm room. Marigold was just getting ready, too, as she tied her hair in her braid.

She was shocked to see Sabrina. And jumped. Sabrina laughed and asked what time they were supposed to meet. Marigold thought and said, "Maybe in two hours." Sabrina opened the door and then headed out of the room. She walked down the hall to her dorm, clicked on the lights, and was surprised to see her mom standing there. It took her a moment to realize that her mom was not upset with her. Sabrina put down her things, and her mom stayed still, sitting on the bed and waiting for her. So she sat down next to her on the bed and asked her what was wrong.

Her mother sighed and paused for a moment before she responded. "Your father has been gone for a long time on a mission. I'm worried about him." Sabrina was shocked. "How long has he been gone?"

"A month. I hope he comes back."

Sabrina was curious. "What mission?"
"Something about a—"

She got caught off as the next bell rang, signaling lunch.

Sabrina got up, waved goodbye to her mom, and opened the door to her dorm. There was a new teacher for her now that she was in the Fifth Level for mastering her power. She went to the fifth floor and ignored the questioning looks from older students. She liked the attention, but this was too much for her. She hung her head down and quickly pushed past the crowd, following the blueprint of the school the principal had given her. She stopped at a door made entirely of glass. She opened it and saw Miles and Simon and Miles sitting on a bench.

The rest of the room had nothing else in it. It was very vacant, and a desk stood in the middle of the room. Simon waved and beckoned for her to come over. She sat down next to him, and he whispered, "I think our teacher is invisible," he said, smiling and pointing to a floating pencil. Miles was practicing helping the flowers grow and was actually pretty good at it. He made one slapping grow into what looked like a kaleidoscope rose. "How are you doing that?" Sabrina asked, fascinated.

"A little trick Mrs. Tira showed me." He laughed. "Pretty useful, actually." "PERFECTO!" a voice said. "I can sense the TALENT! THIS IS ZEE PERFECT SORCERY I'VE BEEN LOOKING FOR! FOR SO LONG."

Sabrina jumped as a man in fancy clothes appeared. She could tell he cared about his appearance. His skin was dark, and his hair was slicked back in a rockstar way. He had golden armbands along his arm and wore a green cloak with the face of a snarling wolf on the front, the mascot, and the logo of the school. He wore designer jeans and had a tattoo on his right arm. Miles mouthed, Is *he talking to me?*

And Sabrina nodded and smiled. Miles blushed and muttered under his breath, "Well—I-I'm not that good." The man frowned. "You got to be kidding me. I see the amazing potential right there in your palm. I know potential when I see one. Nothing will fool me. You wouldn't be upgraded to the Fifth Level if you guys weren't as good as you are." He said, ditching his cheesy French accent. "Anyway," he said, stretching the *A*. One of your moms had a critical meeting to go to and asked me to carry on the lesson for you guys. So . . . Who wants to go first?" He tapped his chin and pointed to Miles. "Ahh, how about the boy over here? Your name?"

"Miles," he said, and stood up. "What would you like me to do?"

The man thought for a moment. "How about you make this kaleidoscope rose turn into a tree?"

Miles frowned and protested. "But, sir, this is a rose. Some plants can't become a tree. Actually, a lot of plants."

The man just nodded and waved his hand as if to say, *Go ahead! Hopefully, you can do the impossible, or else you fail the class for today!* Miles looked at us then at the plant. Then he sighed. "Okay," he said, shrugging as he turned toward the flower and concentrated.

For the first ten seconds, nothing happened. Then, the flower blossomed, and out came another and then another, and another. They twined together and grew ten feet long until it looked like a real tree. It was breathtakingly beautiful, and she swore she saw Miles gasp at his own fantastic well-done job. The teacher stood in awe, as if he knew it wasn't possible, but figured, *Hey? Why not give it a try.* "Im-Im-Impossible! I have never seen something this beautiful in my entire life!" He quickly pulled out his cell phone from his back pocket and took twelve pictures of the tree. "Wow!" he muttered to himself. "Incredible! This is a masterpiece! Pure artwork and dedication! This kid has some skills! Give me a second. I'll be right back," he said and vanished. "Miles, that was awesome, dude!" Simon congratulated. "Give me a high-five!"

"Thanks!" Miles said as he gave him a high five and blushed profusely. He then sat down and willed the flowers down again. "I wonder how I did that," he said. "I'm pretty sure Mrs. Tira didn't teach me anything similar to that." He stared at his wrists in awe. "Wow." Sabrina smiled. She was happy for him. But she was afraid that it was her turn next. What would the teacher think about her skills? Would he doubt them? Would he like them? Worst of all, would he underestimate her? She just needed more time to think.

Too Late.

The teacher appeared back in the middle of the room.

"Ok, shall the lady go first?"

Sabrina nodded shyly and asked him what he wanted her to do.

He thought for a moment and said, "I see you have more potential than any of these students. How about unlocking a new power?"

Sabrina gasped and asked, "What do you mean, unlock a new power?"

The man smirked and grabbed his wand from his desk. He then pointed it at her and muttered a few words under his breath. Sabrina closed her eyes and then opened them again. She felt normal like nothing had happened. She stared at the teacher inquisitively.

"Umm, was that supposed to do anything?" she asked.

The teacher nodded and then said, "I have unlocked your new and final power. Hypnotizing."

CHAPTER EIGHT

Hypnotizing??! Was that even a power in this world? Miles gawked, and Simon stared in awe. The teacher beckoned for her to come forward. When she did, he told her to concentrate and "give it a shot."

Air a second, she thought, *you want me to hypnotize you?*

The teacher must have known what she was thinking because he nodded and closed his eyes as if preparing for an embrace. She figured he wasn't a touchy person at all. Sabrina hesitated. She didn't know what to do. What would she do if she was hypnotizing somebody? It seemed like the million-dollar question at that moment. But, she closed her eyes and concentrated as hard as she could.

When she opened her eyes, the instructor looked the same, except he wasn't closing his eyes anymore—but standing straight and saluting. *At your service, how may I help you?* A voice spoke deep into her head, vibrating her skull. She needed to stop it, and fast.

She closed her eyes and imagined the average rock-star teacher she'd seen moments before, and when she opened her eyes again, he stood there smiling happily and jumping up and down while clapping his hands. "Now that you've proved your excellence, I'll give you one of the Five Elements," he said.

Printed in the United States
by Baker & Taylor Publisher Services